THE WITCH'S CAT

AND THE

COOKING CATASTROPHE

For Jack and Grace. My world. My inspiration.
Love you to the moon and back, and there and back again. xxx

Telltale Tots Ltd.
www.telltaletots.co.uk

First published 2018 by the Independent Publishing Network
This edition published 2020 by Telltale Tots Publishing
Second Edition

ISBN: 978-1-9162549-2-3

A CIP catalogue record for this book is available from the British Library.

THE WITCH'S CAT

AND THE

COOKING CATASTROPHE

WRITTEN BY

KIRSTIE WATSON

ILLUSTRATED BY

MAGDALENA SAWKO

One day, a witch's cat found a dusty old cookbook, and it gave him the most marvellous idea...

"I know," said the cat excitedly, "I will make a super-scrumptious surprise lunch for my lovely witch! How hard can it possibly be!?"

And as he flicked through the pages,

he found the perfect recipe, called...

Witch's Broth

5 fish heads

4 splodges of frogspawn

3 dried lily blossoms

2 drops of dragonfly tears

1 pinch of magic witching dust

Directions: Throw it all in, stir, and leave for 1 minute

"Excellent!" said the cat. "She's a witch and I'm sure she'll like broth. Whatever that is."

Then, he roughly followed the directions, adding an extra sprinkling of magic witching dust for good measure.

"Ha. I'm rather excellent at this cooking thing," he was boasting to himself, when...

Poooffffff!

It was ready!

The mixture was GREEN and gurgling.

The cat took a **BIG** sniff.

"Hmmm. Delicious! But it needs a little something else."

And he knew just the thing...

...SEASONING!

So, he added some herbs and spices, before finishing it off to perfection with a good shake of salt and pepper. "There. Much better!" he said, feeling very pleased.

Just then, The Lovely Witch arrived home.

"Oh Cat! You've made lunch!
What a wonderful surprise,"
she said happily.

"Well, this is interesting," said the witch, as she took
a closer peek at the mixture – which was now
making a funny fizzing sound.

"What's in it? No, wait! Don't tell me.
Let me taste it and guess!"

And with that, she took a
BIG spoonful, swirled it
around her mouth,
then swallowed
with a loud **GULP**, and...

ZAAP!

In a **FLASH** of light,
she turned into...

"Oh **NOOO!**" Cat shrieked. "That wasn't supposed to happen!"
And that's when he noticed an important scribble
at the bottom of the page.

Warning: Adding seasoning to a magic potion will make
it <u>stronger</u>. So, use sparingly. Or ideally not at all.

"A P-P-POTION? Oh no! This isn't a cookbook!"
he realised with horror. "It's a...

...SPELL BOOK!"

"What have I done?! This is NOT good at all. It's a cooking **CATASTROPHE!** And I need to fix it **NOW!**"

So, he searched through the pages of the old spell book,
before deciding to try a new potion called...

Undo Soup

5 cat hairs

4 meaty bones

3 sunny morning dewdrops

2 stinky old slippers

1 pinch of magic witching dust

Directions: Throw it all in, stir, and leave for 2 minutes

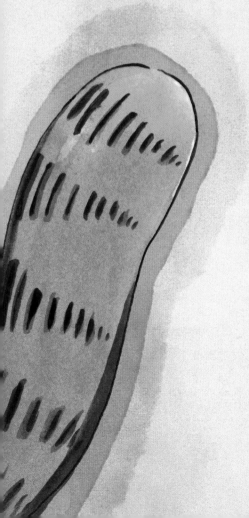

"Hopefully this will **UN-DO** this terrible mess!" he said. Then he set to work on making the new potion. And this time, he was sure to follow the recipe to the very letter.

Well, almost. He could only find one stinky old slipper,
so he threw in some extra cat hairs instead.

"HA! This seems easy enough," he was just thinking, when...

Pooofffff!

It was ready!

The mixture was
BLUE and bubbling.

This time, he resisted adding any seasoning, before serving some up for the frog, and...

ZAAP!

The frog changed into...

...a DOG! "WOOF WOOF!" said the dog.

"Oh, not AGAIN!" said the cat. "I REALLY need to put this right!"

So he flicked back through the book to find an answer.

"Ah! This looks ideal." he said, reading aloud a recipe for...

Make-a-Witch Stew

5 glittery fish scales

4 spindly spider legs

3 tbsps of frog spit

2 sun-ripened pumpkins

1 pinch of magic witching dust

Directions: Throw it all in, stir, and leave for <u>3 minutes</u>

"HA! Hopefully, this will MAKE-A-WITCH this time." he said, as he followed the instructions SUPER carefully. Well, kind of. There was no frog spit, so he used a smidge of dog drool instead.

The cat waited patiently, then...

Pooofffff!

It was ready!
The mixture was
oddly ORANGE.

Once again, he avoided seasoning, before dishing some up for the dog, and...

ZAAP!

The dog magically transformed into...

...a very unhappy witch.

"RIBBID RIBBID!
WOOF WOOF!"

said the witch, crossly.

"Oh dear," said the cat, "I guess it did need frog spit after all!"

Thankfully, the potions EVENTUALLY wore off,
and The Lovely Witch returned to her normal self.

But the cat was **NEVER** allowed to make lunch **EVER** again.

"Ha. She didn't mention **MAGIC** though," he thought to himself,
as he started planning his next magical adventure.

The End.

THANK YOU FOR BUYING THIS BOOK!

I hope you've enjoyed meeting The Witch's Cat. If you have, be sure to check out his other adventures in The Witch's Cat and the Trouble With Tidying Up and The Witch's Cat and the Broomstick Blunder.

Did you know that reader reviews are like **MAGIC** for an author like me? They help bring attention to the book, and help others decide if they'd like to buy it too. So, if you enjoyed this book, please consider writing a review.

Kirstie x

GET YOUR FREE ACTIVITY PACK!

Download from: kirstiewatsonauthor.co.uk/resources

FIND OUT MORE ABOUT KIRSTIE AND HER BOOKS:

 facebook.com/kirstiewatsonauthor

 instagram.com/kirstie_watson_author

YOUR BOOK WAS PRINTED ON DEMAND!

This book was printed on demand by Amazon, which helps minimise waste and is considered more environmentally friendly than traditional off-set printing, since books are produced only when ordered, reducing the need for large print runs and excess inventory.

As the author, I am unable to personally quality check the printed books. However, Amazon provides excellent customer support should you have any queries.

Made in the USA
Monee, IL
21 May 2024

58723555R00024